That's Not Santa!

Story and pictures by LEONARD KESSLER

SCHOLASTIC BOOK SERVICES

NEW YORK · TORONTO · LONDON · AUCKLAND · SYDNEY · TOKYO

ISBN 0-590-32263-X

12 11 10 9 8 7 6 5 4 3 2 1   9   1 2 3 4 5 6/8

Printed in the U.S.A.   07

*For Santa's friends
all around the world*

December 24th . . .

It is the day before Christmas.

Santa's sleigh is filled with toys.

Everything is ready for Santa's trip.

But where is Santa?

He is sleeping.

"Time to get up.

Time to put on my red suit," Santa says.

He looks for his red suit.

He looks everywhere.

"Have you seen my red suit?"

"Have you seen my red suit?"

No one has seen Santa's red suit.

"No red suit.

No Christmas!"

"NO CHRISTMAS?"

"Wait. I have an idea."

"How's this?"

"Oh, no. You can't go out like that.
That's not Santa!"

"Wait. Wait.
I'll be right back," Santa says.

"How about this?"

"Or this?"

"No, no, no.

That's not Santa!"

"Wait. I'll be right back."

"This is it!

Off I go."

"No, no, no.
You can't go out
in your underwear.
That's not Santa!"

Mrs. Claus comes home.

"You can't go out that way.

You will catch a cold."

"But he can't find his red suit."

"Red suit?

Santa, I want you to open

your Christmas present right now."

"A new red suit!

I'll put it right on. Thank you!"

"NOW THAT'S SANTA!"

"It's getting late.

We have to go."

"We?"

"Ho ho ho.

I'm going with you.

I have a red suit too."

"Ho ho ho.

This Christmas will be

twice as much fun!"